MYTHIC ORACLE

WISDOM OF THE ANCIENT GREEK PANTHEON

Messages by CARISA MELLADO
Artwork by MICHELE-LEE PHELAN

SIMON PULSE
New York London Toronto Sydney New Delhi

BEYOND WORDS
Portland, Oregon

SIMON PULSE	**BEYOND WORDS**
An imprint of Simon & Schuster Children's Publishing Division 1230 Avenue of the Americas New York, NY 10020	1750 S.W. Skyline Blvd., Suite 20 Portland, Oregon 97221-2543 503-531-8700 / 503-531-8773 fax www.beyondword.com

First Simon Pulse/Beyond Words paperback edition September 2012

Text copyright © 2008, 2012 by Carisa Mellado
Artwork copyright © 2008 by Michele-lee Phelan

A previous edition of this work was published in Australia in 2008 by Blue Angel Publishing®

All rights reserved, including the right of reproduction in whole or in part in any form.

SIMON PULSE, logo, and colophon are registered trademarks of Simon & Schuster, Inc.
Beyond Words is an imprint of Simon & Schuster, Inc. and the Beyond Words logo is a registered trademark of Beyond Words Publishing, Inc.

For information about special discounts for bulk purchases, please contact
Simon & Schuster Special Sales at 1-866-506-1949 or business@simonandschuster.com.

The Simon & Schuster Speakers Bureau can bring authors to your live event.
For more information or to book an event contact the Simon & Schuster Speakers Bureau
at 1-866-248-3049 or visit our website at www.simonspeakers.com.

Managing Editor: Lindsay S. Brown
Design: Sara E. Blum
Editor: Emmalisa Sparrow
The text of this book was set in Arno Pro.

Manufactured in China

10 9 8 7 6 5 4

Library of Congress Cataloging-in-Publication Data

Mellado, Carisa.
  Mythic oracle : wisdom of the ancient Greek pantheon / messages by Carisa Mellado ;
    artwork by Michele-lee Phelan. — 1st Simon Pulse/Beyond Words pbk. ed.
       p.   cm.
  1. Mythology, Greek—Miscellanea—Juvenile literature. 2. Mythology, Greek, in
    art—Juvenile literature. I. Phelan, Michele-lee. II. Title.
  BL785.M365   2012
  133.3'242—dc23
                                                                                    2012004910

ISBN 978-1-58270-325-1

CONTENTS

Introduction 7
Card Spreads 13

CARD MEANINGS: PROTOGENOI

1. Uranus—*The Father* 21
2. Gaia—*The Mother* 23
3. Pontus—*The Unknown* 25
4. Hemera—*Rebirth* 27

CARD MEANINGS: TITANS

5. Cronus—*Cycles* 31
6. Rhea—*Protection* 35
7. Prometheus—*Sacrifice* 39
8. Mnemosyne—*Inspiration* 43
9. Atlas—*Responsibility* 47

10. THEMIS—*Natural Order*	51
11. SELENE—*Intuition*	53
12. HELIOS—*Illumination*	55
13. EOS—*New Beginnings*	57

CARD MEANINGS: OLYMPIANS

14. ZEUS—*Divine Expansion*	61
15. DEMETER—*Harvest*	63
16. HERA—*Duty*	67
17. HADES—*The Underworld*	69
18. POSEIDON—*Earth Shaker*	71
19. ARTEMIS—*Purity*	73
20. APOLLO—*Clarity*	75
21. PAN—*Nature*	77
22. HEPHAESTUS—*Work*	79
23. ARES—*Battle*	81
24. HESTIA—*Home*	85
25. ATHENA—*Wisdom*	87
26. HERMES—*Messages*	89

27. APHRODITE—*Love*	93
28. EROS—*Desire*	95
29. PERSEPHONE—*Awakening*	97
30. DIONYSUS—*Freedom*	101
31. HEBE—*Play*	105
32. IRIS—*Harmony*	107

CARD MEANINGS: MAGICAL BEINGS

33. CHIRON—*Healing*	113
34. PANDORA—*Hope*	117
35. THE MOIRAE—*Destiny*	121
36. HECATE—*Crossroads*	123
37. THANATOS—*Death*	125

CARD MEANINGS: HEROES

38. ACHILLES—*Glory*	129
39. ORPHEUS—*Faith*	131
40. ODYSSEUS—*The Journey*	133
41. HERACLES—*Strength*	135
42. PERSEUS—*Courage*	139
43. HELEN OF TROY—*Beauty*	141
44. PSYCHE—*Sacred Union*	143
45. BELLEROPHON—*Humility*	147

GLOSSARY	151
ABOUT THE AUTHOR	157
ABOUT THE ARTIST	159

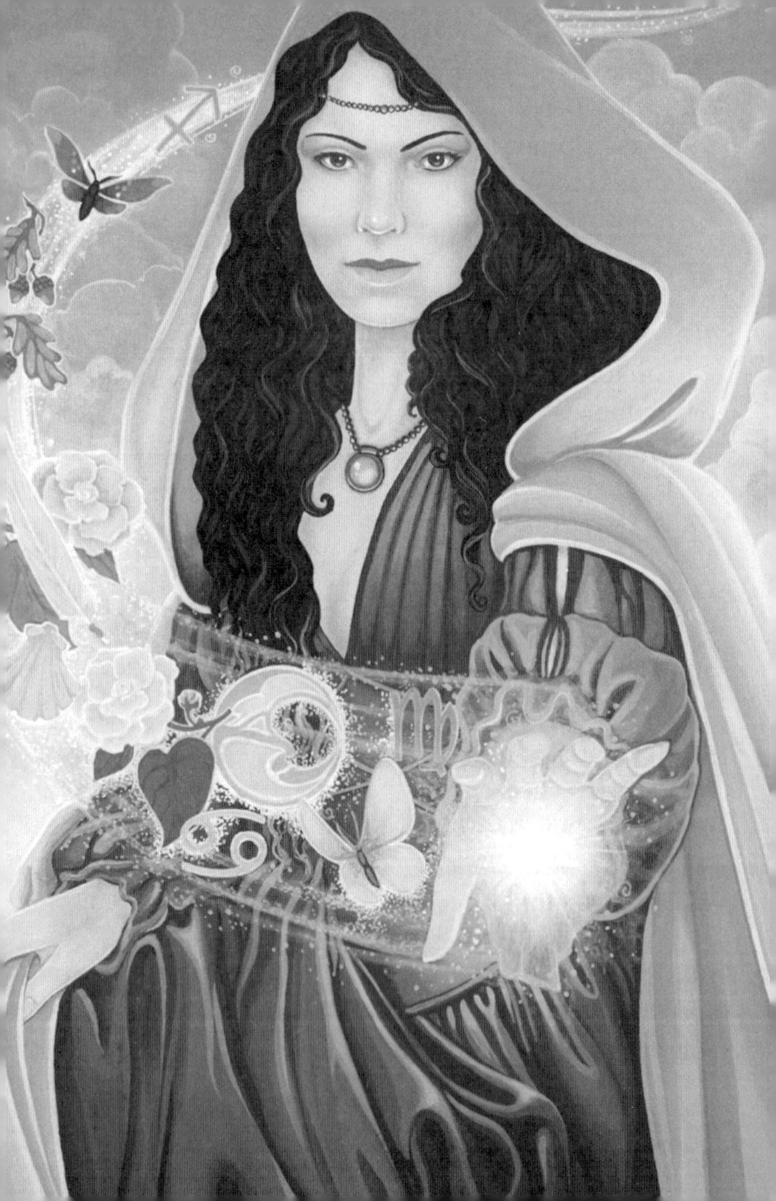

INTRODUCTION

THE GREEK MYTHS are the stories of humankind. They are the stories of human nature, human cycles, and the nature of the divine. It is through the symbols and metaphors of these stories that we come to better understand ourselves and our own internal processes.

These cards are designed to assist in guiding us through the cycles of life, from the larger situations or phases of a cycle to the smaller ones that make up the greater experience of change.

Countless myths essentially tell the same main story (or specific parts of the story), all comprised of the same three main elements that make up what is known as the Hero's Journey—from the departure or the beginning of a journey, to the initiation process, to the hero's eventual return. This journey is a symbolic representation of the cycles of life, and we can use teachings of the myths to assist us in moving through these cycles with awareness and clarity.

The beginning of any cycle or new phase in life always involves an awakening. This may be a totally unexpected call to adventure, whether it relates to love, friends, school, creativity, or personal spiritual awareness. It is here that an interruption in the normal flow of daily life forces us into action. The journey takes us into the unknown, yet we encounter others there who have also taken this journey. They bring unexpected help and guidance as we move beyond the threshold of all we have previously known.

Once we are in new terrain, we encounter challenges. Obstacles test us as we move through the initiation process. We must overcome our fears and face the deepest pit of ourselves in order to move forward. We must go down into our personal underworlds and come back reborn; we must tear away the illusions of our previous selves; we must find a deep union with our new selves and return to the world above with the treasures that we discover. Through these trials and illuminations, we gain new life, new perspective, and a new sense of our selves. We will have faced our fears, dissolved our illusions, and clarified our convictions.

Then begins the stage known as the return. This is the often painful task of returning to the world—we are different, yet the world is the same. We may be tempted to never go back, but if we don't, we will become lost in our own personal labyrinths. This is the time when we must integrate our new selves into the world. It is the time to become master of *both* worlds.

On a more tangible, human level, this process of returning, of reintegration, may relate to our new selves, our relationships, or our activities. It may mean a personal, creative, or spiritual change—a change in our sense of self and how we perceive the world.

When using these cards, read them as a story that tells the journey of you, right now. If you see the cards as a natural flow or story, you will have a greater ability to understand what is happening in your life, what you need, and what comes next.

Each card's message is accompanied by the story and attributes of a god/goddess or hero. It is well worth taking the time to read the stories of these beings, as they will provide you with greater insight when you go on to read the messages they bring you. Think of it as getting to know the storyteller before he or she tells you the story.

The cards in the *Mythic Oracle* are divided into five categories:

Protogenoi

These are the basic essential energies that were born out of creation. They are the original, raw personifications of nature, such as Earth, sky, day, and night.

Titans

The Titans are a race of primordial deities born of Gaia (Earth) and Uranus (sky). The first generation of Titans, led by Cronus, overthrew the rule of Uranus, allowing Cronus and Rhea to become king and queen. They ruled the Earth during the Golden Age, which came before the time of the Olympians. The Titans governed the primal aspects of nature, sun, moon, ocean, Earth, memory, and natural law. Following the great war between the Titans and the Olympians, the Olympians banished most of the Titans to Tartarus, a place in the underworld that is equivalent to hell. In mythology, the Titans reflect the essence of nature and the divine.

Olympians

The first of the Olympian gods were the children of Cronus and Rhea. Led by Zeus, they waged a war on the Titans and succeeded in becoming the new rulers. Zeus and Hera rule the realm of heaven from Mount Olympus, Poseidon rules the sea, and Hades rules the underworld. Although there are twelve Olympian gods in the pantheon, a few of these alternate at different times so that there are actually up to nineteen gods. The Olympian gods tend to reflect nature, as the Titans do—yet the Olympians reflect more clearly the nature of humankind, with each deity revealing different archetypal aspects of humankind. The Titans established the primal aspects of nature, and the Olympian gods added color and detail to the world.

Magical Beings

There are many types of magical beings, some of whom predate the Greek gods and goddesses, humans, and heroes. These beings have unusual origins and natures and fail to fit into simple categories: beings such as Chiron, neither god nor centaur; Pandora, crafted by Hephaestus; the Moirae, otherwise known as the Fates; Hecate, the primordial gatekeeper; and Thanatos, the personification of death.

Heroes

Greek mythology contains countless stories of heroes. Through the stories of the heroes, we learn the universal truths of humankind—how we accomplish, how we love, where love leads us, how we learn to master ourselves, and what natural cycles we experience.

CARD SPREADS

You can read these cards in a variety of ways. No one way is more correct than another. You can change how you read the cards each day, or you can use specific card spreads for specific situations. You may want to experiment with some of the spreads below or even make up your own.

Daily Spread

Pick one card to reflect the general theme for the day. Reflect on the nature of the being represented—pay attention to the message of the card and allow it to guide you throughout the day.

The Nature Spread

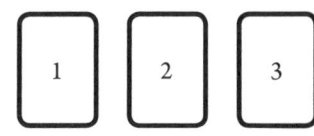

This spread gives you an overview of the larger cycles flowing through your life—past, present, and future. It allows you to see the themes and lessons present in your life. This spread can also be used to look at the energy around a specific situation, project, or relationship. To do this, just keep the situation, relationship, or project in your mind when shuffling and pulling the cards.

1. Past: This card indicates what occurred in your past and the lessons you learned from it.
2. Present: This card highlights what is happening for you now and the lessons you are learning.
3. Future: This card shows you which events, influences, and lessons will arrive in your life.

The Relationship Spread

The Relationship Spread helps you clearly see and understand the relationships in your life. This is relevant not only to love relationships but also to relationships with friends, parents, teachers, and anyone else in your life who is important to you. Focus on one person with each reading of the cards.

1. This card shows the nature of the relationship; how you relate to each other.

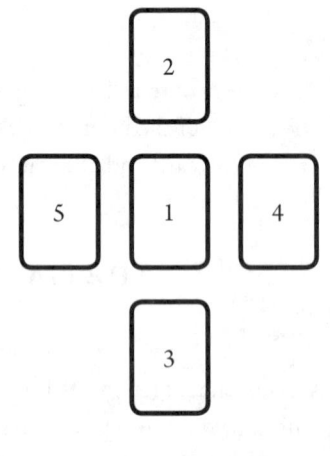

2. This card offers lessons to be learned from the relationship.

3. This card knows the hidden aspect of you that this person reflects. We attract people in our lives who reflect our hidden talents and flaws. When we feel positive toward a person, we are usually attracted to our own unrecognized talents, which we more easily see in others. We may feel negative toward a person because he or she reflects our own unrecognized fears or flaws or what we truly think of ourselves. By looking into this card, learn to heal conflict and own your true potential. Take responsibility for your feelings and your life.

4. This card shows how to bring harmony to this relationship.

5. This card shows what this relationship contributes to your life.

Archetype Spread

The Archetype Spread may be helpful when dealing with issues in relationships or in your general dealings with people. Unlike the Relationship Spread, which focuses on one specific relationship, the Archetype Spread shows you how all relationships are a reflection of yourself and what you can do to bring balance to the situations playing out in your life.

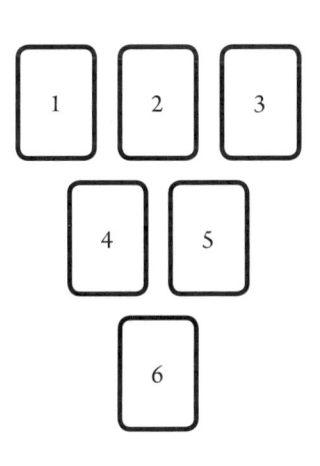

1. **Current archetype:** Learn from this card the energy and themes currently at play in your life.
2. **Personal archetype:** This card highlights your current attitude.
3. **Interactive archetype:** This card shows the archetype you are encountering in others.
4. **What is needed to bring balance:** This card shows the attitude, wisdom, or understanding you need in order to bring balance to your current circumstances.
5. **Sacrifice:** This card suggests the beliefs, fears, or attitudes that you need to surrender in order to grow.
6. **Transformed archetype:** This card shows the outcome of this situation, once the associated archetypes have been transformed.

Cycle Spread

The Cycle Spread may be helpful to use during times of confusion, when it is difficult to see the bigger picture of where you are in your life. It allows you to see meaning and purpose in your current situation and helps you see where things are heading. This spread is also useful when you want to know the correct course of action to take.

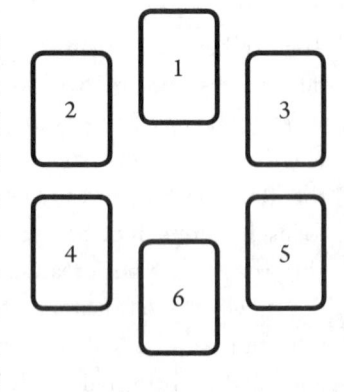

1. **Current cycle:** This card shows the bigger picture of what is currently happening in your life.
2. **Phase in cycle:** This card shows your current place in the bigger cycle.
3. **Heart's desire:** This card shows the deepest needs of your inner self at this time. You must pay attention to these needs, as you are unlikely to progress through your cycle until you have.
4. **Lesson to be learned:** This card shows the gift of your current place in the bigger cycle, what you need to learn.
5. **Freedom to be gained:** This card shows the freedom you will gain when you hear your heart's desire and understand your current lesson.
6. **New beginning:** This card shows the outcome of your successful completion of the current cycle.

HERO SPREAD

```
          ┌───┐
          │ 1 │
┌───┐ ┌───┘   └───┐ ┌───┐ ┌───┐
│ 2 │ │     3     │ │ 4 │ │ 5 │
└───┘ └───┐   ┌───┘ └───┘ └───┘
          │ 6 │
          └───┘
```

The Hero Spread may be useful for issues regarding school, friends, family, travel, or any other major goal you have. It shows you the energy behind your goal, the phase you are at on your journey toward achieving the goal, and the deeper aspects of the journey.

1. Current quest: This card shows your task or goal.
2. Obstacle on the way to your goal: This card shows the fears or illusions that you must overcome in order to meet the current challenge.
3. Hidden gift: This card shows the gift and the wisdom that you already possess but must harness in order to overcome your current obstacles.
4. Magical assistance: This card shows the assistance that is already present around you. This card may also point to unexpected assistance.
5. Initiation: This card shows the deep transformation within yourself and your life that you will experience by meeting this challenge.
6. Treasure to be gained: This card shows the treasure you will find and bring back into the world upon successful completion of your current quest.

Card Meanings
PROTOGENOI

1
URANUS
the father

The Myth

Uranus is the primordial embodiment of the sky. He is the father of the Titans and the partner of Gaia, the Earth. He resented his children and locked the youngest ones away in the center of the Earth. This upset Gaia so much that she convinced her son Cronus to overthrow his father, allowing the Titans to rule.

The Message

Uranus, the father, holds and represents worldly power, as the external world, its structures and power, is the realm of the father. As children, we are born into the realm of the mother. She cares for us as we explore the realms of self, imagination, and feeling—but as we grow up, we must stand and take our places within the world.

The realities of standing in the world can come as a painful shock. We often feel anger, sadness, and frustration as we are torn out of the realm of the mother and forced to take full responsibility for ourselves in the realm of the father, where we may find things cold, terrifying, or overwhelming. But once we reconcile ourselves with the world and take ownership of our lives, possibility becomes available to us. Only when we take responsibility for our lives and truly realize the power that exists within us do we have the power to create the exact lives we desire for ourselves.

This is a time for stepping into and owning your power in the world. What kind of life do you want for yourself? Are you living that life? What can you do to ensure that you are creating that life for yourself every day?

Decide to take ownership of your life today. The only limitations you have are within your own mind. Decide now how to release those limitations, take a risk, and stand in your power.

2
GAIA
the mother

~

THE MYTH

Gaia is the primordial embodiment of the Earth. She is the mother of the Titans and the partner of Uranus. When Uranus began to bury their children at the center of the Earth, Gaia became deeply distraught and convinced Cronus to overthrow his father.

The Message

Gaia represents the fertility of the Earth. Without her care, nothing can grow. She gives us food, warmth, and shelter—the basis for all life—and the safety and physical security necessary for us to thrive. This is the realm of the mother, allowing space for us to explore our inner worlds.

The garden of our lives must be weeded from time to time. Some plants don't live well next to each other, and when we fail to cut off the parts of a plant that are dead, they rob energy and health from the entire plant. Gaia teaches us that when we refuse to let go, life ceases to grow.

Gaia's appearance in your spread indicates that this is a very fertile period for you. Ideas, images, and inspiration are ready for you to plant in your world, and they will bring fruit in the future, with proper care. This card also indicates a connection to something greater than yourself.

This is a time for taking care of school, family, your health, and your personal space. This is a period of nurturing the ground for future growth. Once these areas are stable and secure, you will have the fertile ground necessary for creating anything you want in your life.

3
PONTUS
the unknown

THE MYTH

Pontus is the primordial embodiment of the sea. He is the father of the most ancient sea gods, including Nereus (father of the Nereids) and Keto (mother of the Phorcydes). His partner is Thalassa (spirit of the sea), and together they gave life to the fish and other sea creatures.

The Message

Pontus, the sea, symbolizes crossing the threshold of the unknown. New land and new adventures lie beyond, but first we must surrender ourselves to the all-consuming vastness of life. At the edge of the sea, we experience a sense of awe. A seemingly unending space exists before us with the power to either take us somewhere new or swallow us whole. Ancient in origin, with surfaces that hide strange and unfamiliar worlds, the ocean humbles us with its giant presence.

This is a time for you to cross into the unknown, as all the foundations that have held you until now are crumbling into this oceanic space. You must sail the sea in order to reach a shore.

This may be a frightening, exciting, or overwhelming period where nothing seems certain and the future is unclear, but this space must be crossed in order to reach new land. And remember that no matter how unsettling your journey may be, reaching new land is inevitable.

4
HEMERA
rebirth

THE MYTH

Hemera is the primordial embodiment of day. She is the daughter of Nyx (night) and Erebus (darkness). She is the bringer of the day. At night, Hemera's mother, Nyx, draws the veil of night across the Earth. In the morning, Hemera disperses the night mists and bathes the world in a heavenly light again.

The Message

When we experience a life-changing transformation, we return to a world that has remained the same. Old meanings no longer hold value for us, and we feel a sense of displacement. Although this can be a very frustrating period when the regular world no longer makes sense, eventually we begin to feel new meaning in life, see the sense in things with new eyes, and make the appropriate changes to reflect our new lives.

This is the transformation taking place for you now. You are coming out of the darkness, a life-changing period, and bringing the wisdom from that period into your new life. This takes time, bravery, and exploration. A new you has been born, and you must now give your new self the love and nurturing it needs to grow into its full potential.

This is a period of rebirth. You may have just been through a journey that challenged and awakened you both physically and spiritually. You are surfacing now from the night into the day, changed, and you must reintegrate all that you have learned into your self and your life.

Card Meanings
Titans

5
CRONUS
cycles

THE MYTH

Cronus, son of Gaia and Uranus, is the father of Zeus and many of the Olympian gods. He is a god of harvest and vegetation and carries a sickle. Gaia and Uranus told him that one of his children would overthrow him and, out of fear, he swallowed each child as soon as he or she was born. His wife, Rhea, tricked him when Zeus was born and fed him a stone instead of his newborn, allowing Zeus to be raised in safety. When Zeus reached maturity, he forced Cronus to free his swallowed children, Zeus's siblings. Led by Zeus, they waged war on Cronus until they overcame him.

This is why Cronus represents cycles—although he was a great king, and the period of his reign was known as the Golden Age, it was his fear of cycles and change that led to his eventual demise.

THE MESSAGE

Nature is filled with cycles, including the cycles that exist within our own lives. All things change, and when we embrace and flow with these changes, they enrich both our lives and our experience of life. It can be frightening, but new life is only possible once we accept change.

When we resist the natural cycles of change, we become tyrannical, clinging to the old order. We feel a sense of deadness, followed by bitterness, frustration, fear, and anxiety. When we flow with our changing selves and changing places within the world, we remain connected to life, nature, and ourselves.

This is a time for you to review the cycles in your life. Have you become stuck? Are you trying to hold on to things you should let go of? Are you afraid of moving into the next phase of your life? It may be time to stop, feel the fear, and move forward anyway. Although you may need to let go of your old identity and habits—and this can be frightening—you will find much joy, power, and wisdom when you accept the new cycle. We all fear our mortality, yet it is this fear that leads to our deadening. You will gain a new sense of life when you embrace your cycles with joy, and it is imperative now to mourn the old ways but let them go. Open your arms to the new life and possibilities that await you, and move forward.

6
RHEA
protection

THE MYTH

Rhea is the daughter of Gaia and Uranus. She is the wife of Cronus and the mother of Zeus, Hera, Demeter, Poseidon, Hades, and Hestia. The fertile Earth is her realm. Rhea is also a goddess of mysticism, celebrated through music, dance, and trance. She is the wisdom and mystery of the Earth. In art, Rhea is often depicted on a chariot led by two lions. The swan and the moon are also symbols of Rhea.

Cronus, fearful of being overthrown by one of his children, ate each child as he or she was born. When Rhea birthed Zeus, she fed Cronus a stone instead of her beloved child and hid Zeus in a cave, where he was raised safely in secret. Once he reached manhood, he overthrew his father.

The Message

Rhea represents the protective aspect of the mother. Unable to continue to feed her young to Cronus, she made a dangerous stand against him. She represents the part of ourselves that cannot bear to deny our natural instincts and propels us to do what we know is right for ourselves and the things and people we love. We take a stand against external societal rules and follow our inner ethics instead. This is protection in its highest form—it is the love and protection of what is truly sacred in our selves and in our lives.

This is a time for trusting your instincts and intuition. You may feel torn between your duty to the world and your duty to yourself, but your duty to yourself must always come first. It is your highest priority to protect the sacred life that has been entrusted to you. Bending to the will of peers, media ideals, and other external influences will only leave you drained and powerless. Your own intuition must be the ultimate ruler in your life. You must be the protector of your body, mind, heart, and spirit. Only when you have done this can you have true power and influence in the world. Only at this point can you protect and nurture the things outside of you: your friends, family, schoolwork, or art. This is a time for creating clear and healthy boundaries and honoring your integrity.

Trust yourself and create your life from a place of true honesty and self-love, for if every action you take is rooted in your personal truth, then all that you grow will be golden.

7
PROMETHEUS
sacrifice

THE MYTH

Prometheus is a rebel—a hero and a champion for humankind. When Zeus overthrew Cronus, creating a new world order, he viewed humans as slaves. Prometheus, however, viewed humans as more. He stole fire from the heavens and gave it to humankind. The power to use and control fire meant power, freedom, and independence for humans—the gift of fire brought light, warmth, and food. As punishment for doing this, Zeus had Prometheus hung upside down, and every day an eagle ate his liver. Every night Prometheus's liver grew back, and the process began again.

The Message

A sacrifice for a higher gain is at hand. On a deeper level, we already know this. The necessary sacrifice may be comfort, safety, pride, or the need for instant gratification in the form of money, attention, or approval. We must sacrifice the requests and desires of our egos for a higher cause and a greater gain. We may need to put ourselves in an uncomfortable position for a time in order to reach this higher goal, but the richness of living in our truth and living with integrity will far outweigh any discomfort. To live in this way is to be a true hero.

The myth of Prometheus is about fighting for a higher cause without the promise of fame, riches, or glory. The act is its own reward, and the consequences are acceptable.

What do you believe in? Do you compromise your beliefs so that you can be safe and comfortable? When you contribute to something greater than yourself, do you wait for and expect a reward, or is the act enough for you? Are you willing to maintain your integrity, no matter the cost? What do you need to give up at this time? What is keeping you stuck? Are you ready to live your greater potential?

These are all questions to consider at this time. If you are bored, stuck, too comfortable, or have lost a sense of greater meaning in your life, it may be time to make some firm decisions. If you are currently making decisions, you must reflect on how your decisions will affect others. You need to make a sacrifice for the greater good, and the right path is usually the most uncomfortable yet fulfilling direction to go in. Remember that you will only feel a temporary discomfort during the transition. Even Zeus allowed Chiron and Heracles to free Prometheus once he had served enough time.

Decide to be a hero now and rise above all mundane attachments. Strive to contribute to the greater essence that runs through all things.

8
MNEMOSYNE
inspiration

THE MYTH

The Titaness Mnemosyne, daughter of Gaia and Uranus, is the personification of memory. She and Zeus are the parents of the nine Muses, who are beings of inspiration. Their existence shows that memory and divinity combine to create true inspiration.

The Message

Memories hold all that we know about life and ourselves. Memory is the sacred record keeper of our lives, yet memory and actuality are often different. Actuality is the account of facts, while memory is about how we internalize these facts and how we have experienced our lives, neither being truer than the other.

The divine is the essence of life itself—the universal experience that binds us together—and exists both beyond and within ourselves. It is the consciousness of nature and the cycles of nature: life, death, truth, and love.

When this universal essence blends with your inner realm of interpretation and experience (your personal reality), you receive inspiration. Symbols come to life, sounds open inner doorways, and words become keys to unlocking the otherwise overwhelming experience of life.

If you have drawn this card, then you are being touched by inspiration now. All that you have gathered from your life, as well as all that you feel from life, is awakening in your mind now. New worlds and opportunities are opening up within you.

Make sure you *really experience* what you are feeling now. The inspiration you receive at this time comes from a divine place and speaks of a truth that is not only personal but also universal. Write down ideas and follow them through into actions. New possibilities are opening to you, and you must grab this feeling by the reins and let it take you to new places. Nurture inspiration in your life; surround yourself with things that bring you to life. Spend time in nature, dance, be creative. Above all, listen to the whispers on the wind, for they are leading you beyond the limits of all you've previously known.

9
ATLAS
responsibility

THE MYTH

The Titan Atlas, brother of Prometheus, governed the moon. When Zeus defeated Cronus, he sent most of the remaining Titans to Tartarus, the hell aspect of the underworld. However, he decided to punish Atlas by sending him to the western edge of the Earth to hold the sky up so that Earth (Gaia) and sky (Uranus) could not join again and create more Titans.

The Message

It may feel as though we have the weight of the world on our shoulders, but this is actually due to the lack of responsibility and not the burden of it. When we are truly responsible, we know that we have the power to create whatever we want for our lives.

You have a responsibility, first and foremost, to give yourself a balanced and healthy life, a life that takes care of all your basic needs. It is not your responsibility to carry the burdens of others or to buy into any societal pressures that don't seem relevant to you. In fact, if these types of pressures dominate your life, it is your responsibility to remove them. It is your responsibility to ask for help where necessary and create for yourself the circumstances that will keep all areas of your life balanced. It is not helpful to carry the responsibilities of others or to uphold the expectations of anyone else—if people are never forced to take care of their own needs, they will become crippled. In order to let go of other people's responsibilities, you must let go of your need for approval. Don't seek the approval of others at the expense of your own health.

This is the time to take full responsibility for your life. You alone create your life. You are the victim of no one and nothing. Your life is exactly how you've decided it to be. If things need changing, change them. If old pains and wounds are holding you back, now is the time to surrender them. Give them up now! If that pain is holding you back in life, it is because you are letting it. Decide now to do whatever is necessary to let that old pain go.

You don't have control over the world, but you *do* have the power to take responsibility for your feelings, reactions, and perceptions, and to make empowered decisions about how you live your life.

Now is the time to examine your life and see which areas have become burdensome. It may be necessary to take more time for yourself, ask for help, make schedule changes, stop catering to the needs and expectations of others, or give up your old pain and negative self-talk.

Taking care of yourself is the best gift you can offer the world. You only have one opportunity to live this life, so you might as well make it the best life possible. Taking responsibility for all you experience gives you the power to create the life you want, and only this can lead you to true freedom.

10
THEMIS
natural order

THE MYTH

Themis is the goddess of natural order and justice. The daughter of Gaia and Uranus, she is known for her wisdom and acts as council to Zeus. Themis governs the law of nature, as opposed to the law of humankind. When Themis's order is not respected, Nemesis, the goddess of retribution, punishes the offender.

The Message

Justice is balance, and balance comes with order. Themis is the balance of all things, as is nature. All things have a natural order—day/night, harmony/chaos, birth/death—and when we struggle against this natural order, we become severely out of balance.

This is the time to get your life in order—clear your bedroom and personal space, organize your schoolwork and activities, keep your body clean and healthy, and keep your relationships clear and honest.

Order can take hard work and focus, but it is necessary. It is time to look at all the aspects of your life, on both inner and outer levels, and face them head on. You may need to check your grades or deadlines; confront a person or institution; or deal with personal issues, habits, and beliefs.

We often experience pain and circumstances that feel unfair but, in time, all things find their natural way of returning to balance, and they do not need to be forced. Justice is not "an eye for an eye." Justice is the natural order of the Universe. You cannot control other people, nor can you control every event that happens in your life. You can control your own actions and do what you believe to be right. If you are clear in your life and honest with yourself, then justice surely will follow.

11
SELENE
intuition

THE MYTH

Selene is the daughter of Hyperion (god of light) and Theia (goddess of heavenly light) and the sister of Helios (sun) and Eos (dawn). She is the personification of the moon, often depicted with a half-moon on her head, riding a silver chariot across the sky. She is sometimes depicted bearing a torch.

The Message

This is a time for cutting away all your mind chatter and connecting to the deepest part of yourself. You have an inner voice, a feeling that cannot lie or steer you wrongly. You must be brave enough to hear, acknowledge, and follow that voice. Intuition is not rooted in logical or cultural thought; it is rooted in the deepest core of your being.

If you feel confused or don't know what to do or where to go, realize now that the answers you seek have been within you all this time. You may not be ready to hear them all, but you can hear enough to take you to the next place. You may be on a journey where things need to unfold one step at a time, and your intuition will be the only guide you have along this path. Trust it.

It is important to have a time-out right now, as you must reconnect to your self so that you can hear this inner voice of intuition. It is essential that you write, meditate, or do whatever it is that reconnects you to your self at this time. Intuition is the wisdom of the body, heart, and mind in unison, and outer influences must be cut away at this moment so that you can synchronize with this inner intelligence. You need to establish a routine that includes personal connection time so that you are always in touch with your self.

All the answers exist within you. Right now, all you need to do is listen.

12
HELIOS
illumination

~~~

THE MYTH

The Titan Helios is the son of Hyperion (god of light) and Theia (goddess of heavenly light) and the brother of Selene (moon) and Eos (dawn). The personification of the sun, he is often depicted as a beautiful crowned god who rides a chariot across the sky through the day, illuminating the world with his light.

The Message

When our vision is clear, we have the joy and comfort of perspective—we are able to make sense of past, present, and future, thereby allowing ourselves to make clear decisions about our lives.

If Helios is in your cards today, the sun is shining on you now. This is a time of enlightenment. Clarity and joy will come to you as your life is illuminated.

Things are becoming clear for you, so this is a very good time to write and reflect upon where you are. You may feel yourself brimming with inspiration and positive feelings, as this is an empowering period, filled with vast possibility and much joy. Use this new burst of energy to propel yourself forward to where you want to be in your life but, most important, do not forget to celebrate life, to play and to be merry, for life is nothing without joy.

Now is the time for renewed energy, clarity, and perspective. Have fun, and enjoy this abundant and fruitful period.

13
EOS
new beginnings

THE MYTH

Eos is the daughter of the Titans Hyperion (god of light) and Theia (goddess of heavenly light) and the sister of Helios (sun) and Selene (moon). She is the personification of dawn. Each day, she rises out of Oceanus (ocean) and opens the gates of heaven so that Helios can ride through them and illuminate the sky. She is an incredible beauty, with rosy fingers, golden arms, and large, white wings. She is often depicted as wearing a tiara and a yellow dress woven with flowers.

THE MESSAGE

If you've drawn this card, dawn is here. The long, dark night is over, and you stand at the beginning of a new day. This card comes with a burst of new energy, as all possibility is open to you now. This is a good time to start afresh, make plans, hatch ideas, and open up to your rising inspiration.

The time is right for new beginnings, and you will be projecting this into the world. Don't be surprised if opportunities start knocking on your door—unexpected meetings, gifts, or invitations may turn up. Enjoy this period, and allow yourself to be guided by the Universe and your inner voice. A new day has dawned in your life, so celebrate and enjoy it. A journey awaits you!

Card Meanings
OLYMPIANS

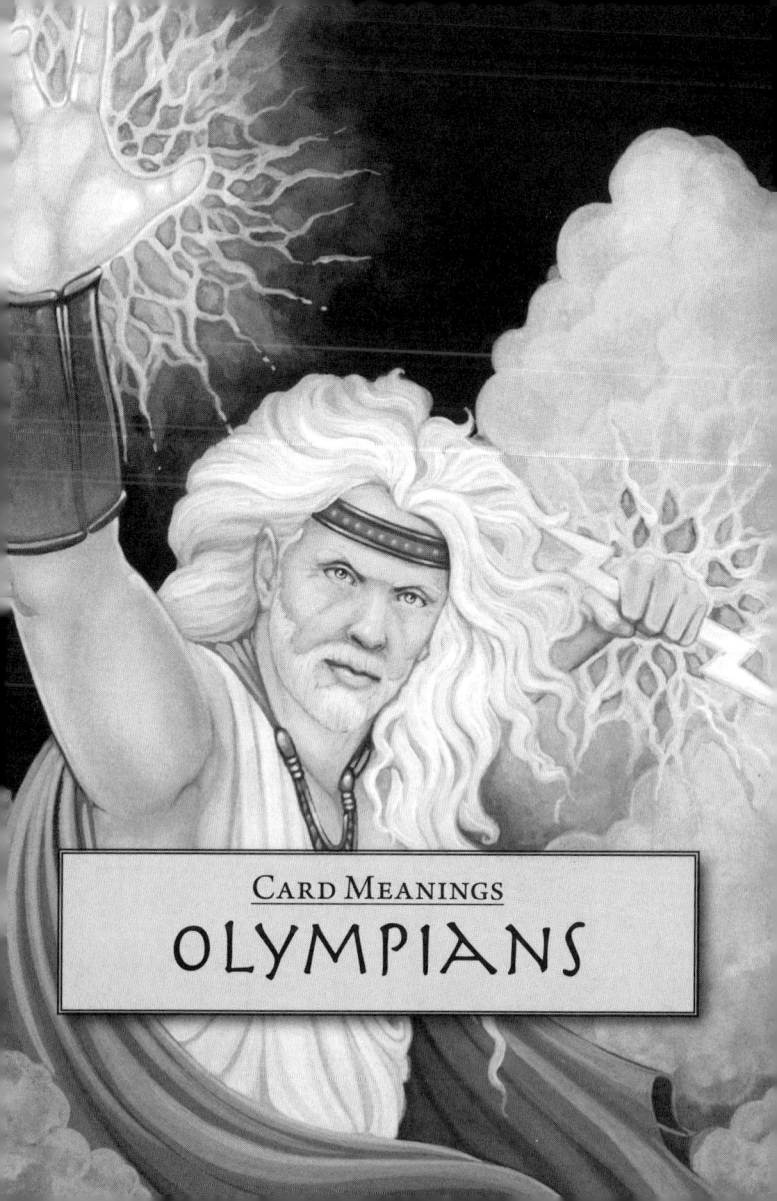

14
ZEUS
divine expansion

~~~~

THE MYTH

Zeus is the king of the gods and the lord of humankind. He is the ruler of the skies and the father of the world. His symbols are the lightning bolt, eagle, bull, and oak. He is the last-born son of the Titans Cronus and Rhea.

When the mortal Semele demanded that he show her his true nature, Zeus revealed himself as pure, intense, blinding lightning, so powerful that it consumed her. As the spirit of the divine spark of life, Zeus fathered many heroes and gods.

The Message

Zeus represents the divine spark of life. He holds the limitless space of the heavens within his realm.

This is a time of great expansion for you. A new spark of divinity has been planted in your life and, as this seed grows, so too does your consciousness undergo a deep transformation and expansion. This may be a good time for you to write or record ideas.

The lightning bolt represents awakenings, realizations, and personal epiphanies, and these can be both joyous and terrifying, as a shift in consciousness always requires you to let go of an old way of thinking. Although your old patterns are now outdated and restrictive, they have also become comfortable, and it takes courage to let them go and to allow yourself to expand.

Lightning touched you and awakened you to your full potential. This is an inspired time when anything is possible. You are shaking off your old, unnecessary patterns and retaining only what is true. As you are electrified by new insights and feel a surge of energy rushing through you, the Universe is guiding you to your higher goals. Trust!

This is the time to live life truly empowered and awake.

15
DEMETER
harvest

THE MYTH

Demeter, goddess of the fertile Earth, is the daughter of the Titans Cronus and Rhea. When Hades stole Demeter's daughter Persephone to be his queen in the underworld, Demeter searched the world in despair and mourned until the Earth became barren. Thanks to Zeus's intervention, Persephone can return to her mother for two thirds of the year, spending one third of the year in the underworld.

This myth explains the changing seasons. When Persephone is away, Demeter grieves and the Earth becomes barren, thus giving us winter. When she returns in spring, new life comes with her. Demeter is happy and the Earth flourishes with life through summer, but things start to die in autumn as the time for Persephone to leave again draws near.

The Message

Our lives always move in cycles. We have periods that are like summer, when everything seems to be flourishing and going well, and periods like winter, when it seems that nothing is working, moving, changing, or improving. Winter may even feel like a period of total mental, emotional, or physical stillness. While every stage of the cycle is important and essential to growth, some stages are harder than others.

If you have pulled this card today, the long and barren winter is over. You may have gone through a period when you were working very hard at school, at home, in activities, or in relationships, with little to no visible evidence for the work you did. That time is now over, and your life is shifting toward movement and rewards.

This is a time of harvest for you. This means that it is time to receive your due for your work. You have been through the harsh, cold winter, worked hard and remained focused, and now is the time for reaping the benefits.

All the seeds that you planted have grown and borne fruit, and this is a time for carefully and lovingly harvesting the fruits of your labor. Within each fruit, new seeds emerge. This is a time of great abundance. Remember to have reverence, humility, and gratitude as you enjoy this joyous part of the cycle of nature.

16
HERA
duty

THE MYTH

Hera, the queen of the gods, is the wife of Zeus and the daughter of Cronus and Rhea. She is the goddess of marriage, childbirth, power, and duty, staying at Zeus's side despite his countless infidelities, though there are many stories of her jealousy and vindictiveness toward Zeus's lovers. Her anger lies at the core of many myths; she creates the challenges many heroes need to face—challenges that, once overcome, end up defining the heroes' powers.

THE MESSAGE

Hera is here to remind us of the realm of duty, but the duty in question is the one toward ourselves and our own personal honor code, as opposed to duty for the sake of status.

When you act out of obligation to others, rather than obligation to your inner self, you begin to lose life force. You become disconnected from yourself and use your senses to discern what action is best in the eyes of the world, rather than doing what you know in your heart to be right. If you give your power, energy, and personal truth away, believing you are helping others, you are really only pursuing status or acceptance for yourself. This can make you angry and resentful. Every healthy person needs a personal honor code, and the courage to stay true to that code is the key to a healthy life.

This is a time for you to check in on your own personal honor code. Are you violating it in any way? Have you disregarded it in order to put the needs of others before your own? This is a time for being honest with yourself. Stand strong in all that you believe.

17
HADES
the underworld

THE MYTH

Hades is the son of Rhea and Cronus. He rules the underworld—the land of the dead. In Greek mythology, the underworld is a vast, complex, and well-guarded landscape. Poets describe it as having many different areas that make up its totality, including Tartarus (an equivalent to hell), the Elysian Fields (reserved for virtuous and heroic souls, similar to heaven), and the Asphodel Meadows (where the indifferent and ordinary souls dwell).

Countless versions of the hero's journey unfold in the underworld. In many myths, the hero takes a trip through the underworld to perform a rescue, take a sacred item, reunite with loved ones, uncover treasures, or resurrect the dead.

The Message

Shadows live in the underworld. All things hidden or lost hide in this realm. One of the most powerful (and usually hidden) feelings all humans harbor is fear, and this subconscious fear often rules our lives. By journeying into the underworld, we can uncover the subconscious drives that rule our lives and bring them into the light so that we can transform them. The treasures we can gain through this process are innumerable, but one of the greatest is self-empowerment.

This is a time for you to be honest with yourself. What is motivating you at this time? Are you living the true essence of your being or are you tricking yourself out of a full life? Sometimes dispelling your illusions and facing your real motivations is horrifying but, by doing so, you reclaim your true power and freedom. The appearance of this card in your spread indicates that you may have been lying to yourself about something, and it is now time to face yourself honestly.

Change is necessary at this time, and going through the underworld will liberate you from your self-imposed chains.

18
POSEIDON
earth shaker

~~~~

THE MYTH

Poseidon is the son of Rhea and Cronus. The ruler of water, seas, and oceans, he is both the supporter of the Earth and the shaker of the Earth—he creates earthquakes by striking the ground with his trident (a three-pronged spear). Poseidon is quite a ferocious god, who demands honor and respect. He is associated with bulls and horses. Bulls were often sacrificed to him to ensure safe ocean voyages, and he is said to have created horses.

The Message

Poseidon is the Earth shaker. If he is dishonored, he is unstoppable in his fury.

The Earth may be shaking for you at this time. Old structures that are no longer useful to you are breaking down, and a new knowledge is removing the foundations on which you've built your current place in life.

The truth is, the old foundations no longer serve you, regardless of whether or not you feel ready to face that fact. They would not have crumbled if they were built on anything that was still truly substantial. The bigger picture may not be in sight right now but, when the time is right, the bounty of a new land will be revealed and it will be up to you to take the next step.

This is a time to clear away outdated thoughts and habits—the old house has burned to the ground, and it is time to build a new one. You may feel sad, angry, or scared—and you must allow yourself to feel all of these emotions—but the truth is, this is an incredibly exciting time full of new opportunities and possibilities. Enjoy it! Ride the waves into a new phase of your life, for adventure awaits you.

19
ARTEMIS
purity

~~~

THE MYTH

Artemis, twin sister of Apollo, is the daughter of Zeus and Leto. She is the goddess of the moon, the wild, nature, and women. Artemis carries a golden bow and arrows, for she is found in the wild parts of the natural realm and is the protector of all that is pure. She is referred to as a virgin goddess because her mind will never be owned by another — she is pure and whole within herself.

The Message

The external world often seeks to civilize us—we learn to work and be productive members of society—but this often comes at the expense of our deeper selves. We disconnect from our raw intuition and instinct and thus become disconnected from life, playing the roles we think we should rather than trusting the deeper wisdom that comes from within. Artemis's presence in your cards today signifies the need for you to return to the wild and natural part of yourself, the part of you that can never be owned.

You may have been acting and making decisions on autopilot rather than focusing on what you need right now in order to restore balance. You may be rather numb and tired, restless, or feeling that there is something missing. There is something missing—you! You probably have been emotionally rooted in the logic of what you can, can't, should, or shouldn't do to the degree that you are no longer sure of the direction of your life. You need to shake up your self-imposed social constraints. Most important, you need to take a risk, whether emotional, mental, physical, or spiritual. You must give up the part of yourself that is not listening to the deeper you. Only when you do that can you take the steps that will bring you back into alignment with your deeper nature and the part of you that will not be owned.

This is a time for releasing external influences and obligations and seeking out the part of yourself that is natural and pure—the part of you that is connected to life and that knows what is right for you, the part of you that is not focused on outcomes but on the journey of life. Here, you find all the answers, true wisdom, and joy.

20
APOLLO
clarity

~~~

THE MYTH

Apollo is the son of Zeus and Leto. He is the twin brother of Artemis and carries a silver bow and arrows. The god of the sun, illumination, clarity, prophecy, art, and music, Apollo had many oracles who spoke his messages to those who traveled to his shrines to hear his wisdom and prophecy. He is also the leader of the Muses and director of their choir. Apollo is a great protector of the people and places he loves. His realm is the realm of light.

The Message

If you've drawn this card, the light of Apollo is touching you. All becomes clear in his light, and this is a time for truly seeing what is, a time for connecting to your personal truth and removing the dust from your eyes and from the corners of your life.

The light of Apollo makes all things shine, and this is a time for getting clear and centered. Apollo's light also brings joy and creativity with it, and you have that great creative power available to you—the power to truly live your greatest potential. This may relate to the kinds of relationships, school environment, or home environment you want for yourself.

You may have just experienced a period of confusion or change in your life that left you with a feeling of being up in the air, not quite adjusted to the transitions that took place, and perhaps not quite sure of where you stand. Apollo comes now to bring light and order to your new life. This is a good time to write, make plans, and establish new routines.

This is a creative time for you. It is time to take a stand for what it is you want for yourself and your life. The old has been cleared away, and a light shines on where you are today. Stand in the light of clear vision and create the life you want to live. The power is yours!

21
PAN
nature

THE MYTH

Although Pan's parentage is unclear, he is usually described as the son of a nymph and possibly Hermes or Apollo. He is half goat and half man. As the wild fertility god of the forest and nature, he represents humankind's base animal nature. Pan has a heavy scent of animal and earth and expresses the raw and wild aspect of nature. Pan is a playful god who is also known for his masterful ability with the reeds we call panpipes.

The Message

This is a time to connect with nature, both your own true nature as well as the wild and natural places of this Earth. What is it that makes you feel connected to your self? What do you love to do? What are you passionate about? What is it that brings you energy and excitement? Let go of your personal insecurities and the judgments of others and allow the part of you that is wild and free to express itself.

This may be a time to take a break from the stresses of life and the process of being productive, both at school and at home. Your soul may be calling you to let go and remember what is beautiful, wild, and free in life. This doesn't mean abandoning all responsibility; it means there is a time and place for everything. When you lose touch with yourself, getting caught in routine, stress, pressure, and duty, you stop seeing what is true and amazing about yourself and life.

Take this time to free yourself from these pressures. Have some fun; do what fulfills you and brings you joy and passion. Connect with nature and the outdoors. Rediscover your own nature, your personal sense of freedom, and your connection to life.

22
HEPHAESTUS
work

THE MYTH

Hephaestus is the son of Zeus and Hera. He was born crippled, but he is Hera's favorite child. The ultimate craftsman, Hephaestus is a sweet and gentle-natured god who created many magical things, including Pandora's jar and Achilles's shield. His creations are filled with magic, life, and wonder. As a divine blacksmith, he is the god of the creative fire.

THE MESSAGE

If Hephaestus has shown up in your cards today, it is a signal that something wonderful will happen when you do the work you love the most. Hephaestus is a craftsman who imbues his work with love, and this is a creative time for you, so focus on crafting and creating true wonders in your life. This does not necessarily relate to just schoolwork, but also to the activities, projects, and passions that you love and choose to put your energy into.

Now is the time to pay special attention to the inspiration you are receiving, for crafting takes a special kind of focus that requires you to be sensitive to the needs of the creation. If you understand that the creation has its own consciousness, you must be willing to craft in service to the creation's needs rather than your own, allowing your work to be filled with magic, life, and wonder.

You may need to put in a lot of hard work, but you will feel passion for and devotion to what you do. This is a magical time of crafting and building. Soon you will need to be a warrior for your work, as you take it boldly into the world.

23
ARES
battle

THE MYTH

Ares is the son of Zeus and Hera. He is the god of war and embodies not only the spirit but also the blood and the guts of the fight. Often thought of as a kind of butcher, Ares does not govern the strategy of war but rather the physical aspect of the fight.

The Message

Ares is here to remind you that you may need to take a step back and see what is occurring in your life. It is dangerous to immerse yourself in the heat of battle without a sense of how and why you are there. It is equally dangerous to remain oblivious to the need for battle when you are in danger of losing your self and your ground.

It may be necessary to fight at this time, but you must understand what you are fighting and why, in order to choose the most beneficial course of action. Fighting for what you believe to be right is very important, but standing for your truth must be more important than achieving your desired outcome. It is very important that you are not fighting just to protect or to nurture an injured ego, as proving that you are right or better is not a noble reason to fight. If that is the reason you are fighting, you need to let the injury go and focus on other opportunities in which to invest your energy.

Also, be careful not to butcher your way through the things and people you love. This is not the way to get things done. If passions are running high, it's important not to take out your aggression on those who love and support you. Sometimes when we can't fight what we are really angry at, we take it out on other targets.

If you have pulled this card, it is time to fight—for yourself, your ground, your loved ones, or your beliefs—but don't fight blindly. You need to understand what is happening and why. Analyze your true motivations. Discover what is driving the battle. After examination, if the battle still seems like it is based on your personal truth and integrity, then move forward with calm, strong action and a clear state of mind.

24
HESTIA
home

THE MYTH

Hestia is the daughter of Cronus and Rhea. Her name means *hearth*, the sacred fire, and Hestia is the virgin goddess of the sacred hearth. The hearth was at the center of families and tribes. Transferring fire from one sacred hearth to another represented continuing heredity.

The Message

This card is all about the warmth and the spirit of the home. It indicates that both home and family are especially important at this time.

Our families are not just our blood relatives, but they are the people who care for and nurture us in our lives and the people for whom we deeply love and care. Our connection to family reminds us of who we are and brings us back to our roots both culturally and personally, giving us a sense of continuity, of being a part of something greater than ourselves. Home is this feeling.

Home is also the ground we create for ourselves: a place of security, peace, and warmth. We rejuvenate ourselves in this place so that we may have the energy to operate in the world.

This is a time for connecting to the nourishing energy of home and family. You can be anywhere in the world to do this; all you need to do is connect to the space within yourself that allows you to feel strong, safe, and warm.

This is a time for creating the right "home" space for yourself. If you feel that your home is contaminated, then you must do whatever is necessary to cleanse it. You cannot hope to operate from a clear space within your life or the world unless you are operating from a clear space within yourself and your home. If you have destructive personalities around you, you must create boundaries and remove these people from your immediate space.

This is also a time to connect to those who are your true heart's family, to those who love you and remind you of who you are.

25
ATHENA
wisdom

THE MYTH

Zeus feared that his first wife, Metis, whose name means *wisdom*, would bear a son who would overthrow him. Zeus swallowed Metis when she was pregnant with Athena. Despite his effort, Athena sprang fully grown from Zeus's head, dressed in her war armor and shimmering gold, holding a sharp spear.

Athena is the virgin goddess of wisdom and appears in many

myths, planning strategies for wars and guiding heroes toward their goals. Her ability to see things from a higher perspective allows her to choose the best course of action.

Athena and Poseidon competed to become the patron deity of what would become Athens. Poseidon created a spring that brought water and trade, but it was salty and not good for drinking. Athena created the domesticated olive tree, which gave the Athenians food, wood, and oil. Her gift was by far the wiser and more fruitful, and she became the patron of Athens, which was named in her honor. This example illustrates how Athena used her ability to see the bigger picture to achieve her desired outcome.

The Message

Athena represents clarity and balance of mind. It may be time for you to stop and take stock of your life. You may need to put feelings to the side and closely review your current situation. You may need to journal, meditate, or go for a long walk in order to obtain clarity.

Athena helps heroes win battles, but only through intelligence, clarity, foresight, and wisdom. This is a time to be smart, and wisdom only comes when the heart and the mind are in balance. If you feel muddled, overwhelmed, or frustrated, it is time to stop engaging in the dramas of your exterior life so that you can see what is really occurring and discover how to move forward and defeat the monsters of your inner life. This is a time to face yourself calmly and honestly, so that the guiding light of clarity can see you through to the next phase in your life.

26
HERMES
messages

THE MYTH

Hermes is the son of Zeus and the nymph Maia. He is an extremely clever trickster by nature and is the divine messenger, delivering messages for Zeus. He is the god of travelers and guides souls traveling to the underworld and the afterlife, which is the realm of Hades. He has wings on his hat, a herald's wand, and sandals. He also invented the lyre (a musical instrument).

Hermes creates the bridge of communication between the worlds. He is the link between god and man, between the heavens, Earth, and the underworld. He is known as a trickster, a thief at the gates, a watcher in the night, and a bringer of dreams. Of all the Greek gods and goddesses, only Hermes, Hades, and Persephone have the ability to travel in and out of the underworld.

THE MESSAGE

Hermes is a trickster and often sends messages in the form of riddles and dreams. When life trips us up, and we find ourselves on strange and perplexing journeys that unravel the mysteries of life and of ourselves, this is Hermes at work.

He might steal something from you and, as you look for it, you may instead discover a whole new world. This is a classic example of how accidents or unpleasant and strange events in life can lead you to your destiny. Countless stories tell of people finding true meaning in life after experiencing illness or loss, or after hitting rock bottom.

Messages surround you right now, but they aren't obvious. They are cryptic and may come in strange ways, but they are there. This is the time to pay close attention to signs and signals. It may be a good time to start a dream journal.

Hermes is also the guardian of those who travel, of those who cross borders and boundaries. These include both the physical borders of home, city, and country and the inner borders of thought, feeling, imagination, and experience.

New worlds are opening up to you. This may be a time for traveling to new places, expanding your horizons, or having other new experiences. It is a time for expanding your awareness through art, music, and literature. Philosophy and history may also expand your personal understanding of life.

If you are restless and feel that there is more to life, more to learn and experience, but you don't know where to start, start where you are! Start the journey now. There are endless worlds to explore, and it is time to open up, investigate new ideas, and cross the borders of what you previously knew to be your reality. There is so much to discover, uncover, and see. The gateways of knowledge and perception are open to you now, so take a deep breath and dive in.

Remain on the lookout, for life is offering you opportunities, but you need to open your eyes and pay attention. It is likely you will be led, in that strange Hermetic way, through the realm of unveiling mysteries and into amazing new worlds of experience, feeling, and thought. You only need to be open and aware. All possibility is present in every moment. Don't get caught up in how the messages come; just pay attention when they arrive.

27
APHRODITE
love

THE MYTH

Cronus, the king of the Titans, came into power by killing and overthrowing his father, Uranus. Cronus castrated Uranus and threw his genitals into the sea. A white foam arose where they fell, and Aphrodite emerged from it, fully grown and beautiful.

Aphrodite, like Eros, has a dual birth myth. Another story describes Aphrodite as the daughter of Zeus and Dione.

The goddess of love and beauty, Aphrodite represents the nature of romantic love and beauty born from both the ethereal and the physical realms. Aphrodite had many lovers and explored the realms of love in great depth. The two myths of her birth express the divine nature and the complexity of romantic love.

The Message

Aphrodite, in her beauty, represents desire and the will to pursue love. She represents the spark that ignites passion, the invitation. If you've drawn this card today, there may be a magnetic energy growing around you.

To connect to Aphrodite is to connect to the powerful forces that propel you forward in love. Of course, you must connect to your divine center of beauty in order to experience this magnetism, and that is also occurring for you now.

This is an exciting, sensual time, when love is "in the air." Whether you are in a relationship or not, this is the time to let go of petty insecurities, past hurts, and any old, tired habits or patterns that have kept you on a romantic merry-go-round.

This is a time to reconnect to spontaneity, imagination, adventure, and fun. The limit of this fun, excitement, romance, and sensuality is restricted only by your own imagination and ability to let go and break free from your fears of intimacy. You will feel every tiny breakthrough as a rush of terror, liberation, or excitement.

This is a time of romantic adventure, so let go, take emotional risks, have fun, be brave, open up, and take the initiative.

28
EROS
desire

THE MYTH

The winged god Eros appears in early creation myths. In the beginning, Eros burst forth from Chaos or, some say, from an egg laid by Nyx. His presence caused all things to come together in desire, including Earth and sky, thus creating the world. Like Aphrodite, Eros has a dual birth myth. A second myth states that he is the son of Aphrodite and Ares. Also known as the attendant to and counterpart of Aphrodite, Eros is the god of desire, love, and beauty.

The Message

Eros holds the seeds of desire and creation within him. He is the personification of beauty. The word *erotic* derives from his name. He represents the almost ethereal and ecstatic state of desire that is evoked within us when we feel a reconnection to nature and the divine, to life and death, to eternity and change rather than the fixed and mundane. Much more than simply the act of sex, eroticism is about being taken out of the mundane; it evokes a sense of union with something greater than ourselves, often speaking to the primal and sublime part of our nature.

This is a magical time when you may be touched by desire evoked by the beauty of life. The seed of creation is a will to connect. You desire to connect with something greater and, through this need, something will be born. It may be a new project or new artistic visions, sounds, words, or ideas. A current relationship may evolve, or a new relationship may be born.

This is a beautiful and exciting time. New life is blossoming from within you. Embrace it!

29
PERSEPHONE
awakening

~~~

THE MYTH

Persephone is the daughter of Demeter and Zeus. One day while Persephone was picking flowers, Hades, king of the underworld, rode his chariot out from the underworld and kidnapped her, taking her below to be his queen. Demeter spent years searching for her daughter, allowing all vegetation to die in her grief. Eventually, Zeus sent Hermes to take

Persephone back to her mother, but Hades tricked her into eating the seeds of a pomegranate. Because she ate the food of the underworld, Persephone must spend a portion of every year in the underworld. Thus, we have winter: Whenever Persephone returns to the underworld, the earth becomes cold and barren.

Persephone may have been forced to become queen of the underworld, but it is a role that she took to very well. She is the caretaker of the dead. She became the mistress of two worlds and holds the wisdom of both within her. She journeys through the underworld and returns to the surface. In a sense, she dies and is reborn every year, like the vegetation that dies and is reborn as the seasons pass.

The Message

Persephone represents the awakening we experience when the mysteries of life open up to us. This awakening also occurs between the innocence of childhood and the realities of adulthood. Persephone's mother, Demeter, held on to her very tightly, and when the gods came to see her, Demeter hid Persephone away, not allowing anyone to get to her. Nevertheless, Hades took Persephone. We cannot escape the awakenings, realizations, and hard truths of adulthood. We all must take that inner journey through the underworld and back. It can be a rude awakening at times, but it is an awakening nonetheless.

This is a time for awakening. You may have recently begun a new phase in your life and felt the wonder and excitement of the new beginning, but now the realities of this new cycle are making themselves known. Things are becoming clearer—that is not always easy, but it is empowering. What you held to be your reality has changed, and it may feel a little like a loss of innocence, but it is important to understand that this awakening represents your growing awareness.

Persephone understands the nature of life and death. All vegetation lives and dies in accordance with her journey in and out of the underworld. Taking the inner journey into the underworld is a scary adventure, but it is time to face yourself, to confront your true nature and the nature of life and death. Through this awakening, you will lose your childish notions and illusions and discover true innocence. Understanding life and death and meeting both with an open heart—this is true innocence.

Allow the mysteries of life to reveal themselves to you—feel them, grieve if necessary, and then open your heart to the truth that comes, so that you can move forward with a greater understanding of life and how to live and create in your world. Your eyes are opening now, and this gives you great power. Use it.

30
DIONYSUS
freedom

The Myth

Dionysus is the son of Zeus and the mortal Semele. While Semele was pregnant with Dionysus, Hera, disguised as an old woman, convinced Semele to make Zeus prove he was a god. Semele asked Zeus to swear an unbreakable oath to grant her a favor. He agreed, and was thus forced to reveal his true nature when she demanded it. Zeus appeared as a bolt of lightning, and its fire consumed Semele. Zeus saved Dionysus by sewing him into his thigh until it was time for him to be born, giving Dionysus two births.

Dionysus is the wise god of nature, vegetation, wine, and music. He embodies the ecstasy and intoxication of unity and the dissolving of barriers. He is known as the liberator, freeing humankind from the chains of the mundane through music, wine, madness, and ecstasy.

The Message

Ecstasy is the transcendence of the ordinary state. It is an altered state of consciousness, a type of trance that moves us beyond our own self-awareness into a unified awareness. This state heightens our thought processes, intensifies our emotions, expands our spiritual awareness, and enhances our physical abilities. Dionysus instigates the trance that ushers us into his realm of ecstatic awareness.

Dionysus represents the freedom of the senses and the liberation of the civil and dutiful mind. His appearance in your cards signifies a deep connection to art, music, and poetry and points you toward obtaining freedom through catharsis.

If your life has become overwhelmed by mundane routine, thought, and existence, Dionysus is here to shake you awake. This is the time for freeing your senses and finding your true voice, your dance. It is a time to break free from the rules of the civil world, to find your own way instead.

If you have drawn this card, liberation is at hand. The key to this liberation will come through deep catharsis—an intense, climactic, emotional experience that leaves you feeling renewed, revitalized, and reborn. The experience will smash the psychological barriers that bind you. This is what the ecstatic realm of Dionysus provides—the experience of religious or spiritual ecstasy, the total experience of unity with all that is, the ecstatic experience of god within and without.

31
HEBE
play

THE MYTH

Hebe, the goddess of youth, is the daughter of Zeus and Hera. She was the cupbearer for the gods and served them ambrosia, the food of the gods. She helped Hera into her chariot, drew Ares's baths, and was the attendant of Aphrodite. She eventually married Heracles after he was granted a taste of ambrosia and became immortal.

The Message

We have the opportunity to experience many things while we are alive, but joy is the only experience that is pure, for it does not serve any purpose other than to honor and celebrate life itself.

If you have pulled this card, the essence of the child is present, and it is time to reconnect to innocence and play. You may have felt yourself becoming tired, serious, and heavy; it is time to relax and let go of the seriousness of the world. Be silly, expand outside your comfort zone, use your imagination, and do things for the sake of fun rather than achievement. All this is essential to your health at this time.

Life can be meant for a lot of things—learning, experiencing, achieving—but none of it means anything at all without fun and play. If you don't nourish this aspect of yourself, you end up feeling numb inside. There is no real point in accomplishing anything in life if you can't feel the joy of it.

Your highest calling right now is to make time for play and celebration. Your spirit is calling you to rise and honor your life.

32
IRIS
harmony

~~~

THE MYTH

Iris is the daughter of the sea god Thaumas and the nymph Electra. She is Hera's personal messenger, able to travel freely through all realms. Represented by the rainbow, Iris is said to provide water to the clouds, and she carries a pitcher of water from the river Styx—the river that creates the boundary between Earth and the realm of Hades. The water from the river has many magical powers. Iris uses it to make those who perjure themselves go to sleep. Like Hermes, Iris carries a herald's wand.

Like the rainbow, Iris is the link between god and humankind, heaven and Earth. Through the unity of sun and water, she creates the full spectrum of colors and brings harmony with her wherever she goes, maintaining communication between the realms.

The Message

If you have drawn this card, it is time to pay attention to your feelings. If you are experiencing conflict in your relationships, it may be time to find out why. Are you happy in your heart? Are you looking after your inner needs? Are you confident and comfortable within yourself? Do you listen to yourself and honor your word to yourself? All of these things directly impact your relationships and your ability to communicate with the world around you.

This is a time for restoring harmony, first to yourself, then to the world around you. This card is about harmony of the heart, and that harmony can exist only when you take care of yourself. This is a good time to write in a journal or sit in a reflective space and focus on what you are feeling and what you need at this time in order to feel nurtured and whole within yourself.

This is the time to find the loving space that exists within your heart and truly open yourself up to love, kindness, generosity, and forgiveness. In order to do this, you may need to take the time to feel love and kindness toward yourself. Only when you have nourished yourself can the abundance of love and joy that exists within you flow out into the world. And it is only then that you will be able to create true harmony with others in a clear and balanced way.

Card Meanings
MAGICAL BEINGS

33
CHIRON
healing

~~~

THE MYTH

Chiron was a centaur—a creature that is half man and half horse. While most centaurs do not have divine parentage, Chiron was born of the union between Cronus (appearing as a horse) and the nymph Philyra. The wise centaur was a teacher to many heroes, including Achilles, Heracles, and Peleus. Chiron was also known as a great healer, but one day Heracles accidentally shot him in the thigh with a poisoned arrow, and Chiron was unable to heal himself. Being immortal, he could not die, but he suffered great pain. Chiron and Heracles convinced Zeus to allow Chiron to give up his immortal life in exchange for the life of Prometheus, whom Zeus was torturing for stealing fire and giving it to man. Chiron was then placed in the sky as the constellation Sagittarius.

The Message

All healing requires a sacrifice of some kind; we must give up that which is keeping us bound in pain, which is usually related to that which is keeping us bound in comfort. Sometimes it feels harder to give up the old, comfortable thoughts and beliefs that are actually keeping us miserable, than it does to be happy and healthy.

If you've drawn this card, you need healing in your life now. Whether you require physical, mental, or emotional healing, you must pinpoint which aspects of your life are in need of balance. This may relate to school, health, or relationships, and you may need to make some active changes in these areas in order to bring them back into an essential state of inner balance. You may need to look over your life and the aspects of it you have not yet owned. You may need to undergo a deep emotional release so that you can facilitate acceptance and forgiveness. A counselor may aid you in this process. Alternatively, there are many books that may be of great assistance to you.

This is a time of healing for you. Chiron informs us that the greatest gifts we impart to the world come from our greatest wounds. Through the process of healing, you can learn about the inherent gifts that exist within you and make the heroic choice to use your gifts for the greater good. The decision to be a healthy person is the greatest gift you can offer the world.

34
PANDORA
hope

THE MYTH

Pandora means "all gifts." Zeus commanded Hephaestus to create Pandora in order to punish humankind for receiving stolen fire from Prometheus. The gods gave Pandora a jar (though she is most often depicted with a box) and sent her to humankind as a "gift." Curious about what the jar contained, she opened it, and all the woes of humankind spilled forth—

hunger, hard labor, disease, and pain—yet hope remained inside the jar.

The Message

Why was hope in the jar with all the sorrows? Is hope the one thing that counteracts all the woes of humankind? Hope is the spark of light that shines inside us no matter what we experience or know about life. To have no hope is to be without reason. Without it, we would probably wither and die—the burden of our inevitable fate would prove unbearable.

Faith is a belief held strong. Hope is a prayer. These are two very different things. Regardless of personal beliefs, hope is the prayer that our lives will have meaning. If we were starving in a desert, hope would drive us on. The moment we lose hope, we die. Hope is our connection to possibility, and that is what keeps us going, no matter what. Without hope, we are defeated.

If you have pulled this card today, you may have been experiencing a period of confusion, frustration, or even despair. You may also have recently experienced a loss of some kind. The loss could be as simple as finding that something you had hoped would be present in your life is not there at this time.

This card is letting you know that we can never truly predict the way things are meant to occur in life. We can only take responsibility for ourselves and how we choose to act. The moment we think we know how something should be, it tips on its head and turns out to be completely different. If something has not worked out for you, it is for one of two reasons: either you are not ready for it, or there is a better way.

Regardless of what is occurring in your life, this is a time of renewed hope. A new feeling will begin to brew inside you, and you may begin to receive signals from the world around you that new opportunity is coming. There is a universe of opportunity available to you, but it cannot be found in the old ways or the old places. This is the time for seeking out new paths, feelings, or ideas and taking new risks.

35
THE MOIRAE
destiny

THE MYTH

The Moirae are beings of destiny, also known as the Fates. Clotho, the youngest, spins the thread of life, deciding when each being is to be born. Lachesis, the middle sister, measures the thread of life, deciding how long each person or being will live. Atropos, the oldest, cuts the thread of life, deciding how each life ends. These three sister crones spin and weave our destinies.

The Message

If you have pulled this card, this is an incredibly magical time for you. Destiny is calling. You may feel prompted to make a leap of faith, unexpected events may occur, inspiration might strike, or you might be about to bring a project to completion. You may even find new romance, receive news about college, become involved in a new activity, or graduation will occur.

Destiny usually brings with it unexpected life-changing events, in which you will find incredible opportunity. These events can come in the guise of something difficult or painful, but do not be fooled—this is a magical time, a culmination of your life so far. It is important to move with the flow. Let your instincts guide you to where you need to be. If you experience painful events, remember to allow yourself a period of grieving, as nothing will feel clear unless you do this.

During life-changing events, it is important that you remain present, clear, and focused. Life often goes through major shifts that are beyond your comprehension and control, but it is still your life, and you control your reactions. Only your willingness to be responsible for yourself will determine how wonderful these changes turn out to be.

HECATE

crossroads

THE MYTH

Hecate is an incredibly important, powerful, and complicated deity. Although she appears throughout Greek mythology, she actually predates it. She is said to be the key-bearing queen of the entire cosmos. Hecate is associated with gateways to hidden realms of existence and is the keeper of sacred knowledge. She is present at the threshold of transformation and represents the road to unknown places.

She is depicted as a triple-faced goddess with the heads of a dog, horse, and bear, or those of a dog, serpent, and lion. She may also appear as a maiden, mother, and crone, representing the passage through the phases of life and wisdom. She is connected to wilderness and wild creatures and is guarded by black dogs. She carries a key, symbolizing her role as gatekeeper, and a torch, which shows that she is one who illuminates and brings wisdom. She brings light to dark places, revealing the treasures hidden in the unconscious. She also carries a knife—which represents power, discernment, and the ability to cut through all things—and rope, symbolizing the cutting of the umbilical cord in birth and the severance of body and spirit in death.

The Message

If you've drawn this card, a major, life-changing crossroads lies before you. Hecate beckons you to choose a direction. You must make a decision. Change is inevitable, but the direction of change is completely up to you. Hecate is calling you to the untamed and wild areas of life. You must follow this deepest of calls. You know the decision you must make—it is probably a terrifying decision, yet it is one that will take you to your highest calling. Do not be afraid of what you feel deep inside. Follow that inner wisdom and let it lead you to your destiny.

37
THANATOS
death

THE MYTH

Thanatos is the personification of death, particularly nonviolent death. He is the son of Nyx (night) and Erebus (darkness) and the twin of Hypnos (sleep). He is believed to have a gentle touch and was seen throughout the Trojan War, carrying off the dead alongside Hypnos.

The Message

Death is a constant part of life—old cells die, and new ones are born. The day comes to an end, and a new one begins.

The appearance of Thanatos in your cards today signifies that a very deep personal transformation is occurring, and you need to surrender something linked with your identity and sense of self within the world. This may be a particular belief system, status, activity, relationship, grievance, or general thought pattern. Whatever it is, it has served you until now, but further progress requires that you release it.

If you feel frustrated with life or the world around you, you may have been directing your attention to the wrong source. What needs transforming now is you. Your life is only a reflection of your innermost fears and beliefs.

You fear losing your sense of self, but death requires you to be larger than the self. The part of yourself you are afraid to lose is based in illusions and rooted in self-importance, identity, and your ego's basic need for comfort and reassurance. The true essence of the self isn't lost after the removal of those ego-based attachments, but rather comes to life once they are released.

Now is the time for you to release your fears and strip away your illusions and ego-based attachments so that you may step into your true essence—your true life.

CARD MEANINGS
HEROES

38
ACHILLES
glory

THE MYTH

Achilles, an extremely complex hero, was the son of the sea nymph Thetis and King Peleus. He was a central figure in the Trojan War, wearing armor crafted by the god Hephaestus. The Greeks could not have won the Trojan War without Achilles.

He was without a doubt the greatest warrior of his time, yet he was also deeply affected by his humanity. He was capable of great love, grief, pride, and an anger that rivaled that of the gods themselves. When Thetis told him that he could either live a long and comfortable life or go to Troy and die with glory, he chose to fight. Despite his skill as a warrior, he was slain. Paris, known as a coward in battle, shot Achilles with an arrow through his heel—the only vulnerable part of his body.

The Message

Achilles accepted his vulnerability, as it is better to die for what you believe in and what you love than to live comfortably without love or courage. Achilles represents our desire for glory and immortality, and the complexity and grief that we find during our search. He accepted the inevitable and yet strove for meaning and purpose. This is the fundamental link that binds all humankind.

If you've drawn this card today, you may be feeling a call to glory, to devote yourself to a higher cause. This is a time to remember that the greatest warrior has the greatest heart. In order to accomplish great things, you must be able to connect to your vulnerability, to reveal something deeper in your nature, to reveal what makes you human. Your vulnerability will connect you to all of humankind and bring power to what you achieve. This is a time to live and breathe the passion that exists within you, for this love and passion will lead you to ultimate glory.

39
ORPHEUS
faith

THE MYTH

Known as the father of song, Orpheus is an incredibly complex mythological figure. He was a master poet and musician and is said to have founded the mysterious Greek religion Orphism.

When a poisonous snake killed his wife, Eurydice, Orpheus journeyed into the underworld to beg Hades and Persephone to allow Eurydice to return to the world above with him. He did this in the form of a song that brought tears to all who heard it—a deep, sorrowful song filled with anguish and longing for his wife. Upon hearing the song, Hades and Persephone were so moved that they granted his request—the only time they ever allowed such a thing to occur. However, they would only allow Eurydice passage back as long as she followed behind Orpheus on their return journey and he did not look back at her until they were safely out of the underworld. Tragically, just before they reached the surface, Orpheus did indeed look back. Eurydice vanished before his eyes and was lost to him.

THE MESSAGE

Why did Orpheus look back? Did he not trust the power of his own song? When we make the difficult journey through the underworld (our subconscious) and undergo the transformation that takes place there, we return to the surface with incredible treasures—but the only way to return with those treasures intact is to maintain faith in our own abilities.

This card shows you have great vision and talent, but it is essential that you believe in yourself, your own song, and the power you hold. You can accomplish miraculous things but you cannot allow self-sabotage and doubt to stump you along the way. You are powerful, and you must now gather the courage and faith to stand in this power. Close your eyes and feel the essence of your being. Breathe into your heart and feel the magic that exists within you. Stand strong in your truth, in your abilities, and in yourself, and you will return triumphant.

40
ODYSSEUS
the journey

THE MYTH

Odysseus was a hero of great wit and intelligence. It was his idea to penetrate the walls of Troy by giving the Trojans a large wooden horse (eventually known as the Trojan Horse) that carried a band of Greek soldiers hidden within it.

After the Trojan War, Odysseus made his way home to Ithaca. While stopping over at an island, he managed to outsmart the Cyclops Polyphemus. Polyphemus, full of rage, asked his father, Poseidon, to never allow Odysseus to reach his home. Poseidon did all he could to prevent Odysseus's safe arrival, although Odysseus eventually returned to Ithaca. Homer chronicled Odysseus's long and arduous journey in *The Odyssey*.

THE MESSAGE

If you've been working toward achieving a considerable goal, this card assures you that you can do it. There will be many challenges along your way. Distractions, temptations, and battles are inevitable in every hero's quest, but only those willing to face the dangers and defeat the monsters experience victory. Those who don't get distracted or give up when the journey gets too rough, those who face every challenge head-on, will assuredly reach their goals. Decide today to be that person. Have heart and courage. Be heroic.

Odysseus fought a ten-year battle at Troy and took another ten years to fight his way back home, but he eventually accomplished the seemingly impossible. Yet it was not the accomplished task that made Odysseus great—it was the journey itself.

This card signals victory. Stay true to your heart and vision now, for you have the power to create and achieve great things. Embrace your journey, both the challenges and the joys of it, and stay true to your heart's desires. Magnificent things are possible now!

41
HERACLES
strength

~~~

THE MYTH

Heracles is the son of Zeus and Alcmene, a mortal woman. Jealous Hera drove Heracles mad, causing him to kill his brother's children. To redeem himself, Heracles offered to serve his cousin, the king. The king set Heracles twelve seemingly impossible tasks to accomplish—tasks that required great strength, courage, humility, and wit to overcome. The tasks were supposed to be his undoing, but Heracles proved himself time and time again, accomplishing every task and acquiring magical items or knowledge with each. Upon completing all twelve tasks, Heracles was free to continue his heroic deeds throughout the land. Heracles eventually married Hebe, the daughter of Zeus and Hera.

The labors of Heracles are all about self-mastery: mastery of the wild beasts within so that a person may use their raw powers in a wise and controlled manner. A number of Heracles's tasks involved killing or capturing wild animals. One of these animals was the Nemean Lion, a creature with skin so thick that it was invulnerable to weapons. Heracles ultimately used the beast's own claws to cut through its skin and was thereby able to defeat it. After this, Heracles always wore the lion's skin as armor.

THE MESSAGE

This card is about strength, focus, discipline, and wisdom. With these qualities, we can harness our own raw powers and use it to create what we want in our lives.

If you find yourself feeling messy, undisciplined, erratic, or caught in any destructive or addictive activity, and your need for instant gratification outweighs everything else, it is time to get organized and take every necessary action to get your life back on track.

This card tells you that it is not enough to act on pure instinct. This is a time for focused strength, self-control, and discipline. This is a time for overriding ego-driven or childlike urges that are often based on a need for pleasure and instant gratification. This is a time for establishing your personal power and learning to govern your life from a place within you that is clear and true. Do whatever is necessary now to take back the power in your life. This is a time for great strength.

42
PERSEUS
courage

THE MYTH

Perseus was the son of Danae and Zeus. King Polydectes fell in love with Danae and wanted to remove her protective son in order to pursue her. Polydectes held a banquet and demanded that Perseus bring him the head of Medusa as a gift. Medusa was a Gorgon—a female creature with sharp fangs and hair of snakes. Anyone who looked upon her face was turned to stone.

Only by using his shield as a mirror could Perseus get close enough to Medusa to cut off her head. From her neck sprang forth the great mythical horse with wings, Pegasus, and the giant hero Chrysaor, wielder of the golden sword.

Medusa represents the deepest fears that hide in the caves inside us, the inner monsters that hold the power to turn us to stone. The head of Medusa represents a mask that, once cut off, allows her to take the new form of Pegasus, who became the horse of the muses. It is said that wherever Pegasus strikes his hoof to Earth, a spring of inspiration flows up.

THE MESSAGE

Perseus is here to remind you of the power that springs forth when you tear off the masks that hide your deepest fears. Those fears cease to be monsters and become magical creatures of inspiration. If you have drawn this card today, you may be experiencing fear in some area of your life that is keeping you paralyzed and unable to make forward progress. The only way to defeat your inner fears is to use a mirror. Face your fears, and they will spring forth as new life from within you.

Fear does not magically vanish because the mind tells it to. Feeling will follow action. It may be necessary to understand where your fear is coming from and why it is not productive to hold on to it. Ultimately, we all have to face our fears, feel frightened, and move forward—only then can we truly allow new feelings and outcomes into our lives. Take action now, regardless of your fears, and life will open up to you.

43
HELEN OF TROY
beauty

THE MYTH

Helen of Troy was also known as Helen of Sparta. She was the daughter of King Tyndareus and Leda of Sparta, though some legends say she was born from an egg after Zeus, in the form of a swan, seduced Leda.

Helen was one of the most beautiful women in ancient times. Her beauty struck Paris, a prince of Troy, with such intensity that he abducted her from her husband, Menelaus. This brought about the ten-year Trojan War.

THE MESSAGE

Beauty is something that can never be defined in a concrete way, as what is beautiful to one person, culture, or period is different to another. Therefore, beauty goes beyond something physical and speaks more about what radiates from within. Beauty is a belief held within a person, an essence and connection to his or her own sensual nature.

Desire and attraction are almost animal instincts. We sense something about someone to whom we are attracted. It is a primal energy. Those who seek to exploit beauty through marketing, for example, will always fail to comprehend its true nature, as marketing speaks much more to the ego, which is all about status and approval, than to the real nature of humankind.

This is a time for you to discard any superficial notions of beauty and connect to the true archetypal essence of what makes you beautiful. *You are beautiful!* All human beings are connected to the same primal beauty, and this beauty is all about the spark within you and what brings you to life. It has nothing to do with your age, hair, makeup, or clothes. The general denial of the primal aspect of human nature has forced beauty into the superficial realm, but it is not beauty that is superficial—it is merely our limited understanding of it.

In pulling this card today, you are being encouraged to connect to the beauty within you and in the world around you.

44

PSYCHE
sacred union

THE MYTH

Psyche was originally a mortal princess, but she ended up becoming the goddess of the soul after completing tasks given to her by Aphrodite. In the myth of Eros and Psyche, Eros's mother, Aphrodite, who was jealous of Psyche's great beauty, ordered Eros to make her fall in love with the ugliest man in Greece. Instead, Eros fell in love with her himself. An oracle told

Psyche's parents she was not destined to be with a mortal man and advised them to place her at the top of a mountain peak. Her parents complied, and a wind carried her away from the peak to a beautiful palace, where she lived with Eros in secret as his wife.

Eros forbade Psyche to look at him and only came to her at night. When her sisters visited, they filled her head with doubts about whom—or what—she had really fallen in love with. During the night, while Eros slept, Psyche crept into the bedchamber with a lamp to see who he really was. Oil from the lamp dropped on him, and he woke up and flew away in sorrow when he realized she had betrayed him. Tormented by grief, Psyche asked Aphrodite to allow them to be together. Still jealous, Aphrodite gave Psyche impossible tasks to complete in order to be with her son again.

Psyche had to sort through a large number of mixed grains, steal golden wool from vicious sheep, fetch water from a river guarded by huge serpents, and go into the underworld and bring back some of Persephone's beauty in a box. Through courage and divine assistance, Psyche completed all the tasks. When Aphrodite still would not allow her son to be with Psyche, Eros begged Zeus for help. Zeus brought Psyche up to heaven and made her immortal, and Psyche and Eros were together again. Aphrodite and Psyche then reconciled.

The Message

Eros and Psyche's story illustrates the exact process every relationship must go through in order to experience true love. It shows what happens when desire falls in love with the psyche (soul). At first, we feel joy, but doubt and mistrust eventually emerge, and personal issues arise. These negative elements could sabotage the union. Like Psyche, we must undergo a rigorous sorting process as we clear away our inner baggage in order to heal our relationships and bring them to a higher place.

This is a period for you to put yourself and your emotions in order. You must face your own fears, sort through your beliefs about love, and truly love yourself and know your own worth. If you clean things up emotionally, you will experience the joy that follows. This process continues throughout your life and the life of each relationship. Some new problem or issue will always crop up, and you must begin again. This is a natural cycle.

It's time to look at yourself and face the fact that you are completely responsible for your relationships. Do you believe you are worthy of love and respect? Unless you can truly love and honor yourself, you cannot have a healthy relationship with someone else. Whether you need to lay better boundaries, be more direct, be less needy and insecure, or be happier and clearer within your own self, it's time to really face up to the negative patterns, beliefs, and habits that have contributed to difficulties in your relationships. Clear those issues out so that your relationships can reach greater heights.

45
BELLEROPHON
humility

~

THE MYTH

Considered one of the greatest Greek heroes, Bellerophon is the son of Poseidon and the queen of Corinth. King Iobates, whose son-in-law was a rival of Bellerophon, sent him on a variety of missions, hoping to kill him. Bellerophon saved the land when he slew the fire-breathing Chimera, a monster with a lion's head, a goat's body, and a snake's tail. He also subdued the violent

Solymi tribe and the Amazons. When the king finally ordered his guards to slay Bellerophon, he killed every guard. At this point, Iobates recognized Bellerophon as the son of a god and welcomed him into his household.

Bellerophon felt that he deserved to fly to Mount Olympus, heavenly residence of the gods, and rode the winged horse Pegasus toward the heavens. Zeus was so offended and enraged by the hero's presumption than he sent a gadfly to sting Pegasus, which sent Bellerophon crashing back to Earth. Bellerophon landed in a thorn bush and lived out his life crippled, miserable, and shunned by men and gods.

THE MESSAGE

No matter how smart and talented, there is not one person alive who knows everything. We all go through life doing our best and using what we have learned from our own experiences and the guidance of others. We all come from the same divine source of energy, but we all have our own unique traits, thoughts, feelings, and experiences. No one is better or worse than anyone else on this planet, and there is something we can learn from every person or event we encounter.

Humility leads to immense wisdom and true power. When you can see the divine in every person and every experience, your life will be blessed and your relationships can flourish. This is a time for recognizing that divinity. What have you learned from your experiences? Sometimes the lesson is simply to know that you should listen to your own instincts or judgments. Sometimes it's about opening to a new perspective. What traits have you had to develop as a result of your challenges? What can you learn from the people in your life?

See the blessings around you now. See the divine in all people and learn from your experiences. Don't allow yourself to be defeated by anything. Allow yourself to grow. Be humble and know that you are a divine and beautiful being of light in a world that is divine and filled with light.

GLOSSARY

Achilles (uh-KIL-eez) great hero whose only vulnerable spot was his heel

Alcmene (alk-MEE-nee) the mortal mother of Heracles

Amazons (AM-uh-zons) race of female warriors

ambrosia (am-BROH-zhuh) the food of the gods

Aphrodite (af-roh-DAHY-tee) goddess of love and beauty

Apollo (uh-POL-oh) god of the sun, illumination, clarity, prophecy, art, and music

Ares (AIR-eez) god of war and battle

Artemis (AHR-tuh-mis) goddess of the moon, the wild, nature, women, and childbirth

Asphodel Meadows (AS-fuh-del) neutral aspect of the underworld where the indifferent and ordinary souls dwell

Athena (uh-THEE-na) goddess of wisdom

Atlas (AT-luhs) Titan who holds up the sky

Atropos (A-truh-pos) oldest Moirae who cuts the thread of life

Bellerophon (buh-LAIR-ah-fon) hero who defeated the Chimera, the Solymi, and the Amazons

Chaos (KAY-os) the infinite space out of which all things were formed

Charon (KAIR-uhn) ferryman of the dead

Chimera (kahy-MAIR-ah) fire-breathing monster with a lion's head, a goat's body, and a serpent's tail

Chiron (KAHY-ron) centaur who was known as a great healer and teacher

Chrysaor (kruh-SAY-or) giant wielder of the golden sword; brother of Pegasus

Clotho (KLOH-thoh) youngest Moirae who spins the thread of human life

Cronus (KROH-nuhs) god of harvest and vegetation

Danae (DAN-uh-ee) mother of Perseus

Demeter (dih-MEE-ter) goddess of the fertile Earth

Dione (dahy-OH-nee) mother of Aphrodite

Dionysus (dahy-uh-NAHY-suhs) god of nature, vegetation, wine, and music

Electra (ih-LEK-truh) sea nymph; mother of Iris

Elysian Fields (ih-LEE-zhun) heaven aspect of the underworld reserved for virtuous and heroic souls

Eos (EE-os) goddess of the dawn

Erebus (AIR-uh-bus) primordial god of darkness

Eros (AIR-os) god of desire, love, and beauty

Eurydice (yoo-RID-uh-see) wife of Orpheus

Gaia (GAHY-uh) the Earth; mother of the Titans

Gorgon (GOR-guhn) female creature with sharp fangs, hair of snakes, and the ability to turn others to stone with a look

Hades (HAY-deez) god of the underworld

Hebe (HEE-bee) goddess of youth

Hecate (HEK-uh-tee) gatekeeper of hidden realms and sacred knowledge

Helen of Troy (HEL-uhn) woman of renowned beauty whose abduction by Paris caused the Trojan War

Helios (HEE-lee-os) god of the sun

Hemera (HEM-air-uh) primordial goddess of the day

Hephaestus (hi-FES-tuhs) god of creative fire; divine blacksmith

Hera (HAIR-uh) queen of the gods; goddess of marriage, childbirth, power, and duty

Heracles (HAIR-uh-kleez) great hero renowned for his strength and the completion of twelve impossible tasks

Hermes (HUR-meez) divine trickster, messenger god, and god of travelers

Hestia (HES-tee-uh) goddess of the hearth and the sacred fire

Homer (HOH-mer) Greek epic poet; author of *The Odyssey*

Hyperion (hahy-PEER-ee-uhn) god of light; father of Selene, Helios, and Eos

Hypnos (HIP-nos) personification of sleep

Iobates (ahy-OB-uh-teez) king who sent the hero Bellerophon on a variety of missions

Iris (AHY-ris) goddess of the rainbow, messenger of Olympus

Ithaca (ITH-uh-kuh) home of Odysseus

Keto (KEE-toh) primordial sea goddess who mothered a host of monstrous children known as the Phorcydes

Lachesis (LAK-uh-sis) middle Moirae who measures the length of the thread of life

Leda (LEE-duh) mother of Helen of Troy

Leto (LEE-toh) mother of the twins Artemis and Apollo

lyre (LAHY-r) stringed instrument like a U-shaped harp, invented by Hermes

Maia (MAHY-uh) nymph and mother of Hermes

Medusa (meh-DOO-suh) Gorgon who was beheaded by Perseus

Menelaus (men-ah-LAY-uhs) Greek king who declared war with Troy over the abduction of his wife, Helen

Metis (MEE-tis) mother of Athena

Mnemosyne (nee-MOS-uh-nee) goddess of memory

Moirae (MEE-ruh) three elderly crones who weave destinies; also known as the Fates

Muses (MYOOZ-ez) beings of inspiration; traditionally, there are nine

Nemean Lion (NEE-mee-uhn) invulnerable lion defeated by Heracles

Nemesis (NEM-uh-sis) goddess of retribution

Nereids (NIR-ee-ads) sea nymphs

Nereus (NEER-ee-uhs) sea god; father of the Nereids

nymph (NIMF) spirit of nature usually associated with a particular location or landform

Nyx (NIKS) primordial goddess of night

Oceanus (oh-SEE-uh-nuhs) god of the ocean

Odysseus (oh-DIS-ee-uhs) hero of great wit and intelligence who fought in the Trojan War; envisioned the Trojan Horse, which ultimately allowed the Greeks to win

The Odyssey (OD-uh-see) epic poem describing Odysseus's ten-year journey as he attempted to return home after the Trojan War

Olympian (oh-LIM-pee-uhn) any god who resides on Mount Olympus

Olympus (oh-LIM-puhs) the home of the Olympian gods

Orpheus (OR-fee-uhs) master poet and musician known as the father of song

Orphism (OR-fism) a mysterious Greek religion started by and named after Orpheus

Pan (PAN) half goat, half man; god of the wild

Pandora (pan-DOR-uh) woman created by Hephaestus; opened a jar and let out all the woes of the world

pantheon (PAN-thee-on) collective group of gods

Paris (PAR-is) prince of Troy who abducted Helen of Troy

Pegasus (PEG-uh-suhs) winged horse that sprang from Medusa's body

Peleus (PEE-lee-uhs) father of Achilles

Persephone (per-SEF-uh-nee) queen of the underworld

Perseus (PUR-see-uhs) great hero who slew Medusa

Philyra (fi-LAHY-ruh) nymph; mother of Chiron

Phorcydes (FOR-sid-eez) group of monsters (including the Gorgons) birthed by Keto

Polydectes (pol-ee-DEK-teez) king who sent Perseus to fetch the head of Medusa

Polyphemus (pol-uh-FEE-muhs) cyclops who was defeated by Odysseus

Pontus (PON-tuhs) the primordial embodiment of the seas

Poseidon (poh-SAHY-duhn) god of the sea

Prometheus (pruh-MEE-thee-uhs) Titan who stole fire from the gods and gave it to humans

Protogenoi (proh-toh-JEN-ee) group of primeval deities born at the beginning of the universe

Psyche (SAHY-kee) wife of Eros; goddess of the soul

Rhea (REE-uh) Earth goddess

Sagittarius (saj-it-TAIR-ee-uhs) constellation created when Zeus placed Chiron in the sky

Selene (sih-LEE-nee) goddess of the moon

Semele (SEM-uh-lee) mother of Dionysus

Solymi (SOL-ih-mee) tribe of fierce fighters defeated by the hero Bellerophon

Styx (STIKS) river that creates the boundary between Earth and the realm of Hades

Tartarus (TAHR-ter-uhs) hell aspect of the underworld

Thalassa (thuh-LAS-uh) spirit of the sea

Thanatos (THAN-uh-tos) personification of death

Thaumas (THAW-muhs) sea god; father of Iris

Theia (THEE-uh) goddess of heavenly light; mother of Selene, Helios, and Eos

Themis (THEE-mis) goddess of natural order

Thetis (THEE-tis) sea nymph; mother of Achilles

Titan/Titaness (TAHY-tuhn/TAHY-tuhn-es) race of deities born from Gaia and Uranus

Trojan Horse (TROH-juhn) hollow wooden statue of a horse in which Greeks concealed themselves in order to enter and defeat Troy

Trojan War (TROH-juhn) ten-year war fought between Greece and Troy

Troy (TROY) city that fought a war with the Greeks over the abduction of Helen of Troy

Tyndareus (tin-DAIR-ee-uhs) king of Sparta; father of Helen of Troy

underworld (UHN-der-wurld) land of the dead

Uranus (YOOR-uh-nuhs) the sky; father of the Titans

Zeus (ZOOS) god of sky and thunder; king of the Olympian gods

ABOUT THE AUTHOR

CARISA MELLADO is an Australian author who has spent more than a decade studying many different aspects of the Mind, Body & Spirit field and also has worked for many years as a professional tarot reader. She has a strong interest in psychology and world spiritual traditions and is an expert in the area of mythology.

She is the cocreator, with Toni Carmine Salerno, of the bestselling *Ask an Angel* oracle cards.

Carisa is also a singer/songwriter. As well as releasing her own musical projects, she has composed music for several meditation CDs. Carisa also runs the Mystical Lights, a spiritual website at themysticallights.com, where many meditations, articles, and spiritual courses are available.

ABOUT THE ARTIST

MICHELE-LEE PHELAN has been painting since the year 2000. In her teenage years, many told her a career in art was an unattainable dream; some actively discouraged it. But Michele-lee believes that some dreams are more than just dreams; they are destiny, and it was her destiny to become an artist. Self-taught, she has spent the years since then learning and refining the necessary skills and techniques, and developing her bold, colorful style. It is a style that has become recognizable regardless of the medium used and the subject depicted.

For this artist, her art is the key and the genre of fantasy is the doorway. Both have led Michele-lee to explore realms real and imagined. A painter of dragons, mythology, goddesses, and faeries, her works also often echo her spiritual beliefs. Fantasy and faith are intimately entwined.

Her artworks and prints now grace the walls of many homes throughout the world. Each is a reflection of the magick she feels and creates and the care and pride she takes in creating both her paintings and her merchandise. Attention to quality and detail are of paramount importance.

As a professional illustrator, Michele-lee has completed the cover artwork and internal illustrations for many publications, including the *Oracle of the Dragonfae* by Lucy Cavendish.

You can visit her website at dreamsofgaia.com.